Mr. Stumpguss Is A Third Grader

KATHLEEN DUEY lives in an avocado and persimmon grove with her husband and her two sons. She thanks the people who have taken on the hard work of passing on the torch of civilization—our schoolteachers. Shine when you can, trudge when you have to. Your work is so important to all of us.

Mr. Stumpguss Is A Third Grader

KATHLEEN DUEY

Illustrations by Gioia Fiammenghi

MR. STUMPGUSS IS A THIRD GRADER is an original publication of Avon Books. This work has never before appeared in book form.

AVON BOOKS
A division of
The Hearst Corporation
1350 Avenue of the Americas
New York, New York 10019

Illustrations by Gioia Fiammenghi
Published by arrangement with the author
Library of Congress Catalog Card Number: 92-90564
ISBN: 0-380-76939-5
RL: 1.6

First Avon Camelot Printing: November 1992

Printed in the U.S.A.

OPM 10 9 8 7 6 5 4 3 2

To Steven, Seth, and Garrett.
You are my sunshine.

CONTENTS

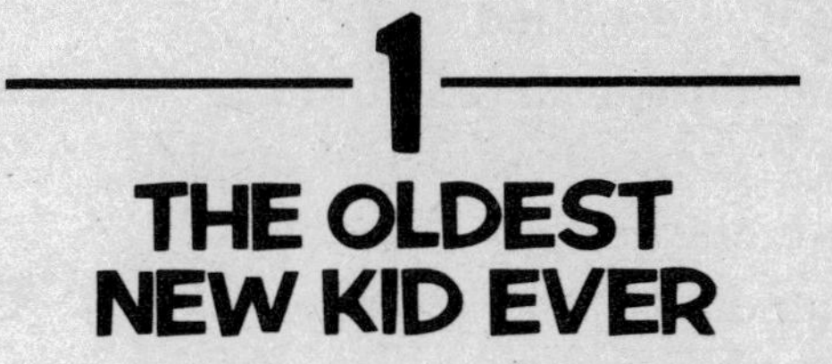

1
THE OLDEST NEW KID EVER

Seth was always a little late starting for school. It was okay. Ben and Tuck were always late, too.

Besides, Seth liked to run.

Seth saw Ben at the corner. Ben was eating an apple.

"Want to race?" Seth called. He looked both ways and crossed the street. He jumped up on the curb.

Ben shook his head. He almost never wanted to run.

"Tuck will race you," Ben said. He pointed.

Seth looked down the street.

Tuck was coming out of her house.

Her real name was Adrian Tucker. Seth never called her Adrian, though. No one did—unless they wanted to make her mad.

"Race?" Seth called. "I'll beat you to the steps."

Tuck waited for him.

They got lined up.

Seth looked back at Ben. He was chewing a big bite of apple. His cheeks were all puffed out. He swallowed the apple and nodded. "Ready . . . set . . . GO!" he yelled.

Seth and Tuck started running. Tuck got ahead when they went around the corner.

Seth ran harder.

He crashed through some bushes. They tore across the playground.

Tuck jumped over the end of the slide.

Seth ducked under the jungle gym.

Tuck beat him to the steps.

"You won," Seth panted.

Tuck smiled, pushing her curly brown hair out of her eyes. She usually won, but she never bragged about it.

The bell rang.

Seth looked for Ben.

He was coming. He was eating a banana now. He was walking a little bit faster.

"Move it, Ben," Tuck yelled. "Or you'll be late again."

Ben trotted toward them, his backpack bouncing on his shoulders. They waited for him. Once Ben got there, they went inside.

The second bell rang.

The halls weren't very crowded. Almost everyone was already in class.

They turned into room 27.

Mrs. Fox was at the blackboard. Seth liked her a lot. He had been worried about third grade, but Mrs. Fox was making it fun.

Ben and Tuck both sat in the front row. Seth sat in the back row.

Seth started toward his desk.

Then he stopped.

He couldn't believe what he was seeing.

Yesterday the seat across from his had been empty.

Today there was someone in it.

But it wasn't a new kid.

An old man was sitting in the desk. He had on a black suit. His hair looked like silvery cotton. He was turning a black hat around and around in his hands.

The old man wasn't smiling. His eyes looked kind of big and watery behind his glasses.

In fact, he was frowning.

Seth tried to stop staring, but it was hard.

The old man looked silly sitting in the desk. Was he a third grader? How could there be a third grader with white hair?

How many times would you have to be held back to be a hundred years old in the third grade?

Seth started to laugh, but he covered his mouth.

His laugh came out in little snorts.

"Please sit down, Seth," Mrs. Fox said. "You're distracting everyone."

Seth looked around. No one was looking at him.

They were all staring at the old man.

"Please, Seth," Mrs. Fox said.

Seth walked to his desk and sat down.

Now the old man was staring straight ahead at the blackboard. He kept turning his hat in circles.

He was way too big for the desk.

His knees were out in the aisle.

"The Senior Citizen Center has sent us a helper," Mrs. Fox said. "Mr. Stumpguss will be here until lunch recess."

A few of the kids giggled.

Seth looked up at Mrs. Fox.

When she didn't want anyone to act up her lips got stiff. He watched her smile get smaller. Her teeth disappeared.

There.

Her lips were stiff.

The kids got quiet again.

Seth looked back at the old man.

His name was Mr. Stumpguss?

What a funny-sounding name.

There was a loud crinkly noise from the front row.

"Put your lunch away now, Ben," Mrs. Fox said. Somebody laughed. Seth could see the back of Ben's head. His ears looked bright pink.

"Let's get right into our reading groups this morning," Mrs. Fox said.

She had her hands on her hips. Her lips were still pretty stiff. Like puppet's lips.

"Reading groups," she repeated.

There were five round tables at the back of the room, one for each reading group.

Kids were finding their reading books and moving to the back of the room. It was noisy.

Seth dug his book out of his desk. Some papers fell on the floor.

They slid across the aisle.

Mr. Stumpguss bent over and picked them up.

He handed the papers to Seth.

"Thanks," Seth said.

Mr. Stumpguss had wrinkly hands. His knuckles were bumpy. He didn't smile.

Seth pushed the papers back into his desk and got moving.

Mrs. Fox had let them vote on names for their reading groups. Seth's group was called the Bobcats.

The Bobcats sat at a table near the windows.

Tuck was a Bobcat.

So was Ben.

There was another boy named Dana Yen.

Seth sat down.

Dana leaned over and whispered, "Is he going to be here every day?" He pointed at Mr. Stumpguss.

Seth shook his head and lifted his shoulders. "I don't know."

Mrs. Fox was looking at the Bobcat table.

"Best behavior, please, everyone," she said.

She used her important voice.

It was deep and slow and smooth.

It was the voice she used after her lips got stiff.

"Mr. Stumpguss will help the Bobcats read this morning," Mrs. Fox said.

Mr. Stumpguss was turning his hat around again.

He was frowning.

Seth knew why Mrs. Fox had told Mr. Stumpguss to help them.

The Bobcats were the worst readers in the class.

Seth tried to read better.

But it was hard.

Reading was the only thing Tuck *wasn't* good at.

She hated it.

Dana and Ben read so slowly that Seth almost went to sleep before his turn came.

Mr. Stumpguss walked to the back of the room.

Tuck and Ben were whispering.

They looked up when Mr. Stumpguss pulled out the extra chair.

He sat down between Seth and Dana.

Mr. Stumpguss wasn't very tall, Seth thought. But he was too big for the chair.

His knees stuck up.

"Don't mind me," he said softly. His voice was scratchy and quiet. He smelled like peppermint. He set his hat on the table.

The hat looked funny sitting there.

It had a wide black band of ribbon around it. The ribbon wasn't shiny. It had perfect, skinny little humps, all lined up.

There was a greeny-purple feather under the ribbon.

The feather was a little crumpled.

"Let's get started, Bobcats," Mrs. Fox said.

Her lips weren't stiff anymore. She was smiling and her voice was back to normal.

Seth opened his reading book.

Mrs. Fox came over and gave Mr. Stumpguss a book.

"Just help them on a word if they get stuck," she said. "It's the story titled 'For Abby.' " She smiled again and walked away.

Mr. Stumpguss opened the book. He pushed his glasses higher on his nose.

READER
3

He turned the pages slowly, then stopped.

"Not that story," Dana said.

He showed Mr. Stumpguss the right page.

"Well, get going, get going, don't mind me," Mr. Stumpguss said. He picked up his book and held it up high, looking at the page. Seth looked at his bumpy knuckles while Tuck started reading.

She got stuck on a hard word.

Mr. Stumpguss looked over the top of his book at her, frowning.

But he didn't help her.

Seth watched Mr. Stumpguss.

Why wasn't he helping Tuck? It was mean not to help her.

Tuck figured out the word and went on.

Seth kept watching Mr. Stumpguss.

He was staring at his book again.

His eyes were going back and forth, and he was moving his finger on the page.

He was still frowning.

But he didn't look mean.

Mr. Stumpguss looked worried.

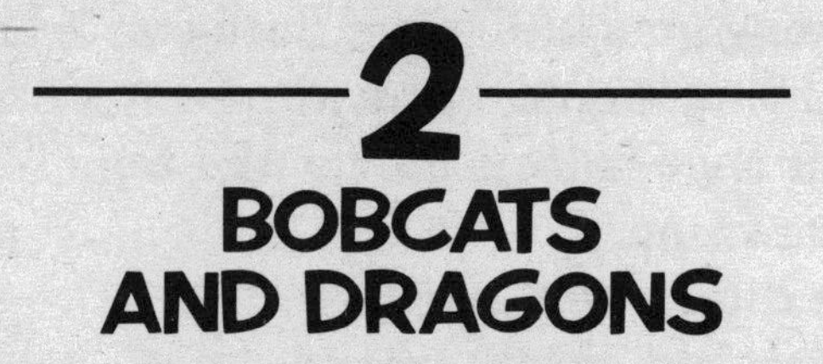

2 BOBCATS AND DRAGONS

Wednesday, Mrs. Fox brought in two big paper bags and set them by the door.

Seth sat up straight at his desk.

Mrs. Fox always thought of fun things for them to do.

Seth looked back at Mr. Stumpguss.

He wasn't in the empty desk today.

Mrs. Fox had brought a folding chair for him to use. He was sitting in the back of the room.

"Would you help me, Mr. Stumpguss?" Mrs. Fox asked.

Mr. Stumpguss got up and set his hat on the chair seat. He walked to the front of the room.

He took one of the bags and carried it to Mrs. Fox's desk.

She carried the other one.

"We're going to make animals," Mrs. Fox said. "Animal shapes, I mean. By gluing these on paper."

Seth leaned out of his desk to see better.

Mrs. Fox was taking big jars out of the bags.

There were jars full of beans, and jars of rice and oatmeal and sunflower seeds.

There were lentils and peas, too. And something tan that Seth wasn't sure about.

"Sesame seeds," Mrs. Fox said as she set the jar down. "Like on hamburger buns."

Mrs. Fox had colored paper, too.

"Let's use our reading tables," she said.

Seth got up and went to the Bobcat table.

"I'm going to make a dragon," Ben said.

"I'm going to make a horse," Tuck said. "A horse rearing up. Or maybe one running." Tuck always made horses. Her notebook was full of horse drawings.

"I think I'll make a big fish," Dana said.

Mr. Stumpguss walked around, passing out the paper.

"First, draw an outline of the animal," Mrs. Fox said. "Then glue the beans and seeds down. Use them for feathers or fur or scales. A big bean could be the animal's eye."

Mrs. Fox filled paper cups with beans and seeds.

Mr. Stumpguss brought them the cups.

He made sure everyone had glue.

Seth looked at his paper.

What he really wanted to make was a bobcat.

But he wasn't sure what a bobcat looked like.

"Be sure you don't use too much glue," Mrs. Fox reminded them.

Mr. Stumpguss brought his folding chair to their table.

He sat down, holding his hat. He wasn't turning it around in his hands. He was leaning forward, looking at the cups full of beans and seeds.

"I want to make a horse," Tuck said again.

Mr. Stumpguss smiled. He looked very different when he smiled. He looked much nicer.

His eyes got crinkled up.

His teeth were white and perfectly straight. Seth looked at them. Maybe they were fake teeth. Dentures.

His grandmother had dentures.

"Do you like horses?" Mr. Stumpguss asked Tuck.

Tuck nodded. "I love horses. I want one."

"When I was a boy I lived in Colorado," Mr. Stumpguss said. "On a ranch."

Tuck lifted her chin. "Really? Were you a cowboy?"

Mr. Stumpguss chuckled. "Not really. Not like the movies. We rode everywhere, though. Had to.

My father was a stubborn old coot. Never would buy a car."

Tuck's eyes were shiny. "Did you ride your horse to school?"

Mr. Stumpguss nodded, but his smile was gone. "I rode everywhere, like I said. Now get to your beans and seeds, young lady."

He pointed at the paper cups.

Tuck was staring at him.

"Get to it," Mr. Stumpguss said again. He was frowning a little.

Seth looked down at his paper.

Mr. Stumpguss was friendly, then he was grumpy. He never helped when they got stuck reading.

Seth wasn't sure he liked Mr. Stumpguss very much.

"What are you going to make, Seth?" Mr. Stumpguss asked. He took off his glasses and rubbed them on his shirt.

Seth looked up. "I'm not sure. Maybe a bobcat."

Mr. Stumpguss nodded. "Bobcats are pretty. Those brown beans are about the right color, too."

Seth stared at Mr. Stumpguss. He looked friendly and nice now. "You've seen a bobcat? A real one?" Seth asked.

Mr. Stumpguss nodded. "They can run like blazes. We used to come upon them when we moved the cattle up to the spring pasture. Here, let me show you."

Mr. Stumpguss put his glasses back on. He got a piece of paper from the middle of the table.

Seth looked at Ben and Dana.

They weren't working yet, either.

They were watching Mr. Stumpguss.

So was Tuck.

"I'll need a pencil," Mr. Stumpguss said.

Seth handed him his pencil.

Mr. Stumpguss bent over the paper. He drew fast, swooping the pencil around.

"There you go," he said. He turned the paper around and slid it toward Seth.

Seth stared at the paper.

There was a drawing of a bobcat. It was perfect.

It looked like a picture out of a book.

"Wow," Dana said softly.

Tuck looked at the paper, then up at Mr. Stumpguss.

Ben's mouth was open.

"You're really good at drawing," Tuck said.

"Always did like to draw," Mr. Stumpguss said. He was smiling. "Now you use that to look at and draw a bigger one on your own paper."

"You're really good," Tuck said again. The picture was amazing. Perfect. The bobcat was snarling.

Mr. Stumpguss raised his head and looked around. "Get to it. Don't want Teacher mad at us for being slow, do we?"

They all started drawing and gluing.

Mr. Stumpguss helped them. He showed Tuck how to make a horse's legs look real.

He helped Dana make a fierce dragon.

All their animals turned out really well.

Mr. Stumpguss's hands were sticky with glue when they were finished. He took a white handkerchief out of his pocket to clean the glue off.

Mrs. Fox put their papers on the counter by the sink to dry.

"These are just lovely," she said. "Just lovely. Now wash up and let's read."

They got in line and washed their hands.

Then all the kids got their books.

"I'll go first," Tuck said. She was smiling at Mr. Stumpguss.

Tuck read pretty well. She didn't get stuck.

Then it was Ben's turn.

Ben read slowly. He always did. He almost got stuck once. His face turned pink.

Then he figured out the word.

When it was Seth's turn, he read his page, then looked up. Dana started reading.

Seth watched Mr. Stumpguss.

Mr. Stumpguss was holding the book up high like he always did.

It was almost touching his nose.

His finger was sliding back and forth.

He was frowning again.

He looked worried when he frowned.

Seth's elbow bumped his pencil.

It rolled off the table onto the floor. He had to get out of his chair and go under the table to get it.

When he got up, he could see Mr. Stumpguss's book.

Mr. Stumpguss was still sliding his finger under the words.

Seth could even see his eyes moving back and forth.

But Mr. Stumpguss was on the wrong page.

3
WORRIED

The Wednesday after that, they did another big art project.

This time Mr. Stumpguss helped them make animals out of reddish clay.

Tuck made a beautiful horse.

Seth made another bobcat. It was pretty good.

Dana made an octopus. Ben made a duck.

Mr. Stumpguss made a grizzly bear.

It was so good everyone in the class kept coming over to watch him.

Then they cleaned up the clay and started reading.

It was a story about a man named Tiko. He made pots and bowls and plates out of clay.

In the story, Tiko was running out of clay.

He couldn't go and look for more because something was wrong with his legs. He had a daughter named Risha. Risha wanted to go look for clay.

Her father said no.

He thought she might fall in the river and drown.

She went anyway, to help him.

She didn't find any clay, but she saved two other kids from drowning.

Dana read the last part. He got stuck on a word in the last sentence.

Mr. Stumpguss frowned and peeked over the top of his book.

Tuck whispered the word to Dana.

Dana finished the story.

At the end of the story, Risha's father said she could go look for clay by the river again.

He said that she was growing up.

Seth liked the story. It was good.

"Write three sentences," Mrs. Fox said. "About why you liked the story, or about why you didn't like it."

Seth borrowed paper from Ben.

Dana borrowed a pencil from Ben.

Ben always had lots of everything.

"What are you going to write?" Mr. Stumpguss asked Seth.

"I liked it," Seth told him. "I liked the girl."

"I did too," Mr. Stumpguss said. "Risha was very brave."

He had closed his book.

He was tapping it with his fingers. He was frowning again.

Seth couldn't figure it out.

Mr. Stumpguss wasn't mean.

He was nice.

He helped everyone with art projects.

He told stories about his ranch in Colorado sometimes. Everybody liked him a lot.

But he never helped when they had trouble reading.

Maybe Mr. Stumpguss was thinking about something else while they read.

Seth's mother did that sometimes. She acted like she was listening, but she wasn't.

"Risha was really brave," Tuck said. "She saved those kids."

"It's just a dumb story," Dana said. "A girl couldn't really do that."

Mr. Stumpguss had been holding his hat on his lap.

Now he set it on top of his book and leaned forward.

"Well now, Dana, that's where you're wrong," he said. "My sister saved a girl from drowning once."

Tuck looked at Dana, lifting her chin high.

Dana always said girls couldn't do things.

It always made Tuck mad.

Tuck looked at Mr. Stumpguss. "Tell us how she did it."

Mr. Stumpguss smiled. "Just jumped right in." He tapped his finger on his hat. "We grew up on the river, so we both swam like trout. She just pulled the little girl right up on the bank."

He stopped and rubbed his cottony hair. "The girl was from town. Was out on a picnic with her folks. None of them could swim a lick. My sis was a hero that day."

"Wow," Tuck said. "I wish I could do something like that."

Mr. Stumpguss smiled wider.

Seth liked it when he smiled.

His eyes were all crinkly.

His teeth were shiny white.

"Well," Mr. Stumpguss said to Tuck, "you'll get your chance. Just be brave."

"I will," Tuck said.

"Me, too," Seth said.

Mr. Stumpguss turned to smile at him.

"I liked the part when the girl climbed down the rocks to get to the river," Ben said.

Mr. Stumpguss nodded. "That was a good part."

"I liked it when her father was all worried and then she walked up and she was fine," Seth said.

Tuck kept smiling at Mr. Stumpguss.

She really liked him, Seth could tell.

She always walked out to his car to say good-bye when he left at lunch recess.

"Well now," Mr. Stumpguss said. "Get to your writing."

Tuck pushed her hair back and bent over her paper.

Seth started writing too.

"How do you spell *swimming*?" Ben asked.

Mr. Stumpguss didn't answer.

Seth looked up.

Mr. Stumpguss was looking at the book again.

He hadn't heard Ben.

"S-W-I-M-M-I-N-G," Seth told Ben. He *thought* there were two M's, anyway.

He looked at his book. There were two. Good.

Ben wrote the word down.

"When you're finished, return to your seats," Mrs. Fox said. "I have a great story to read to you today."

It got noisy while they went back to their desks.

Mr. Stumpguss sat at the back of the room.

Seth put his book away and scrunched down in his desk chair.

He liked it when Mrs. Fox read to them.

She made different voices for the people in the story.

She yelled when the people in the story yelled. She whispered when they whispered.

This one was a funny story.

Mr. Stumpguss laughed when Mrs. Fox read the funny parts.

Everyone was laughing.

When the story was finished, Mrs. Fox looked over everyone's heads at Mr. Stumpguss.

"You know what would be fun?" she asked.

Seth twisted around to look at Mr. Stumpguss.

He was smiling, and shaking his head. "No. What?"

Mrs. Fox was leaning forward in her chair.

She looked excited. Her eyebrows went up when she was excited.

"It would be fun to find some stories Mr. Stumpguss heard in school," she said, looking back at the class.

Mr. Stumpguss was nodding, but he wasn't smiling anymore.

"I know the librarian will help me find an old reader," Mrs. Fox said. She clapped her hands. "Mr. Stumpguss could read a story to us."

Kids cheered.

Seth really liked Mrs. Fox, but he felt angry at her.

He wasn't sure why.

Maybe Mr. Stumpguss wouldn't want to read in front of everyone.

He seemed kind of shy, like Ben was.

Ben hated doing problems on the board, or anything like that.

Seth saw Tuck looking back from the front row.

She looked like she was about to cry.

He wriggled around in his seat to look at Mr. Stumpguss again.

Mr. Stumpguss was turning his hat around and around in his hands.

He was frowning.

But he didn't look mean.

He looked worried again.

The bell for first recess rang.

Everyone got up and went to line up to go outside.

Tuck didn't get in line. She went to the back of the room.

Seth saw Tuck talking to Mr. Stumpguss.

They both looked worried.

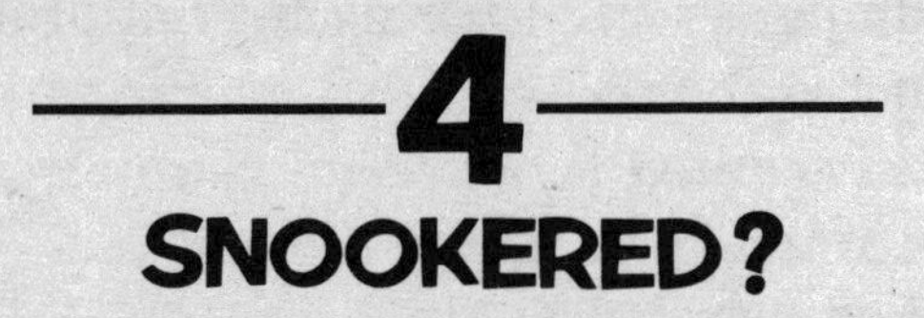

4
SNOOKERED?

On Friday they did another art project before reading groups. It was fun.

Mrs. Fox gave them waxed paper and some broken crayons.

They folded the waxed paper and put little pieces of crayon inside.

Then they used an iron to melt the crayon pieces. They put the waxed paper under a towel, and ironed the towel.

The colors ran together.

"Looks like church windows," Mr. Stumpguss said.

His had mostly red and blue in it.

Mr. Stumpguss helped hang the waxed papers on a string in front of the windows. The colors looked beautiful in the sun.

During reading Seth kept looking at the colors. He lost his place twice. Tuck helped him find it both times. Tuck was reading better and better.

They played monsters at first recess.

Tuck didn't play. She talked to Mr. Stumpguss.

After recess they did math problems on a worksheet.

When the bell rang for lunch recess, Seth went to the door and lined up with everyone else.

Mrs. Fox walked them down the hall.

Mr. Stumpguss walked with her.

He always went out with the class.

He always talked to Tuck for a few minutes.

Then he got in his car and drove away, waving at everyone.

Seth liked Mr. Stumpguss's car.

It was black.

It had big round fenders. It had a huge, fat steering wheel.

When they got to the doors, kids started running.

Seth followed Ben and Dana outside.

They ran all the way across the playground to the big maple tree.

"Want to play the monster game again?" Dana yelled.

"Sure," Ben said. He had brought an apple to eat during recess.

They ate lunch right after recess.

But Ben could never wait for lunch.

"Who'll be the monster?" Ben asked. His cheeks were full of apple.

"Let's get Tuck," Seth said. "She'll chase us."

They looked around for Tuck.

Then Seth saw her back by the building.

"There she is," he said.

"She's still talking to Mr. Stumpguss," Dana said.

"He'll leave in a minute," Ben said. He was almost finished with his apple.

Seth looked at Mr. Stumpguss and Tuck. Tuck was laughing. Mr. Stumpguss had his hat on. His cottony hair poked out from under it. He was cleaning his glasses on his shirt.

"Last one there has to be the monster if Tuck won't," Dana yelled.

They all started running.

When they pounded up behind Tuck, Ben grabbed her arm. "Come be the monster," he said, pulling her around.

She twisted away.

"Not now. Shhh." She waved her hands at them.

"Then the last one back has to be the monster," Dana yelled.

Seth watched Ben and Dana run back toward the tree.

Dana was winning.

Seth decided not to follow them.

"My sister rode in that horse race when she was just a little thing," Mr. Stumpguss was saying. "I guess she was about twelve."

Seth looked at Tuck.

She was shaking her head. "Twelve isn't little," she said.

Mr. Stumpguss smiled.

"I guess not," he said.

"Did you have a lot of horses?" Tuck asked.

"Some years we did," Mr. Stumpguss told her. "Maybe thirty at a time. Sis and I had to break the horses for the ranch."

"Like in a rodeo?" Seth asked. "When they buck and everything?"

"No," Mr. Stumpguss said.

He shook his head. "First you gentle a horse, Seth. Talk to it. Lead it around. Get it used to things. Do it right and they don't even buck when you finally get on."

"I wish I had a horse," Tuck said.

"Me, too," Seth said. He hadn't ever really thought about it before.

Mr. Stumpguss told them about a horse that loved to jump over things. Her name was Lucky.

Lucky had jumped over fallen logs, just for fun, when she was in the pasture. So Mr. Stumpguss had trained her to jump over fences.

"Never had to open gates after that," he said. "Lucky would just jump us right on over."

"Did Lucky ever buck?" Seth asked.

Mr. Stumpguss was leaning against the brick wall of the school building.

The breeze made his cottony hair move.

"Not Lucky, no," Mr. Stumpguss said. "But we had a colt once . . . a year-old colt that was stronger than a grown horse. We tried to train him."

Some kids ran past.

Dana and Ben were both being monsters.

Everyone was yelling and screaming.

Seth wished they would stop.

He couldn't hear Mr. Stumpguss.

Tuck waited for the kids to go past. "Did you ever ride him?" she asked Mr. Stumpguss.

Mr. Stumpguss nodded and smiled again. "Sort of." He was looking out over Tuck's head. "It's a long story, that one," he said. "Too long for now. It's time for me to go home."

"I wish you could stay all day," Tuck said.

She kicked at the grass.

"Don't fret," Mr. Stumpguss said. "I'll tell you Monday. I got snookered into this. May as well stick with it."

Mr. Stumpguss patted Tuck's head.

Then he reached out and grabbed Seth's shoulder.

Seth jumped a little.

"Stay out of trouble, you two," Mr. Stumpguss said.

He waved and walked slowly toward the parking lot.

"Let's go and be monsters," Seth said.

Tuck watched Mr. Stumpguss drive away.

Then she nodded.

They ran.

They ran after Ben and Dana. Tuck caught both of them. She caught other kids, too. She was the fastest runner in the third grade.

The warning bell rang.

They lined up, waiting to go in and eat lunch.

"I wonder what *snookered* means," Tuck said.

Seth shook his head. "I don't know."

They went down the hall toward the cafeteria.

Mr. Stumpguss had said that on Monday he would tell Tuck the story about riding the colt.

Seth wanted to hear that story.

5
SECRET KEEPERS

"I wonder where Tuck is," Ben said as they walked to school on Monday.

Seth shrugged. "I don't know. Maybe she's sick."

Ben shook his head. "Tuck almost never gets sick."

Ben was eating an orange.

He had to walk bent over so the juice wouldn't run down his shirt.

Seth kicked pebbles along the sidewalk. It felt funny to walk all the way to school, instead of running.

They got to the steps just as the second bell rang.

Room 27 was noisy. It was always noisier on Mondays.

Mrs. Fox said they all had to get back into the swing of school after the weekend.

Mr. Stumpguss was sitting in his folding chair at the back of the room.

Tuck wasn't sick.

She was already there.

She was talking to Mr. Stumpguss.

"Happy Monday," Mrs. Fox said in a loud voice.

Kids laughed and groaned. Dana pretended to throw up.

"Reading groups first today," Mrs. Fox said.

Seth went to sit at the Bobcat table.

The story was about a boy who lost his friend's dog.

Dana had trouble with a word. He looked at Mr. Stumpguss.

"That's easy," Tuck said quickly. "It's a com . . . compound. It's two words put together—see?"

Dana looked back at his book.

"Oh," he said. "It's *doghouse*. I get it now."

Seth stared at Tuck. She had been reading better and better lately.

Now she sounded like a teacher.

Dana finished his page.

Seth took his turn.

Then Tuck read, then Ben.

Ben read slowest.

When they finished their story, they went back to their own desks.

Tuck said something to Mr. Stumpguss when she stood up.

Seth couldn't hear what she said.

Mr. Stumpguss patted Tuck's shoulder. He winked at her. Then he sat down in his folding chair.

Mrs. Fox started reading a story.

Mr. Stumpguss laughed at the funny parts.

He laughed louder than anyone.

When Mrs. Fox was finished, she closed the book and looked up.

Seth could tell she was looking at Mr. Stumpguss.

"The librarian has found an old textbook for us, Mr. Stumpguss," Mrs. Fox said. She was smiling. "Maybe next week you could read out loud to the kids?"

"I can't do it as well as you do," Mr. Stumpguss answered.

His voice sounded different.

Seth turned around and looked at him.

He was turning his hat around and around.

Seth turned back to look at Mrs. Fox. She was still smiling.

Her eyebrows were way up.

"I think the kids would love it," Mrs. Fox said.

Everybody cheered.

Seth turned around in his desk.

Mr. Stumpguss was smiling, too. But it didn't look like his usual smile.

His eyes weren't crinkly.

It was like someone had glued a smile on his face when he was really worried.

Seth looked back at Mrs. Fox. She was holding up a book. The cover looked brown and old.

"You can look through it, Mr. Stumpguss," Mrs. Fox said. "Pick a story. Even a short one would be terrific."

"Well," Mr. Stumpguss said. "Well. All right."

His voice still sounded different.

His hat was going around and around really fast.

"Wonderful," Mrs. Fox said. "Let's do it."

She put her hands flat on her desk and leaned toward the class.

"Wouldn't you like to have Mr. Stumpguss read you a story that kids read when he was in school?"

"Yeeessss," the kids yelled.

Everyone liked Mr. Stumpguss now.

He always helped with art projects.

He was nice to everyone, too.

Mrs. Fox nodded. She looked happy. She loved it when the whole class was excited about something.

The bell rang.

It was time for recess.

Kids ran down the hall, even when Mrs. Fox told them to slow down. Seth ran, too.

Then he remembered Mr. Stumpguss's story

about the big colt. He stopped at the bottom of the steps and waited.

Kids were running for the swings.

Seth saw Ben on the merry-go-round. He was eating a banana.

Dana ran past. He hit Seth's back on his way to the merry-go-round.

Mr. Stumpguss was talking to Mrs. Fox.

She was handing him the old book.

Then he started down the steps, holding the railing.

He was frowning. Tuck was right behind him.

Seth followed them over to the fence.

"We'll think of something," Tuck was saying to Mr. Stumpguss.

"Might be smarter if I just stopped coming," Mr. Stumpguss said.

Then he saw Seth. He said hello.

Tuck turned around.

"Seth can help us," Tuck said. "He can keep a secret."

Seth looked at her. "What secret?"

"Can I tell him?" Tuck asked Mr. Stumpguss.

Mr. Stumpguss looked at Seth for so long it made him feel strange.

"May as well tell him," Mr. Stumpguss finally said. "He's about got it figured out now."

Seth shook his head. "I don't know what you're talking about."

Tuck was pulling him closer.

He could smell Tuck's wool sweater and Mr. Stumpguss's minty smell.

"Mr. Stumpguss can't read," Tuck whispered.

Seth shook his head. How could that be true? All grown-ups could read.

Then he remembered how Mr. Stumpguss had been on the wrong page.

He remembered how Mr. Stumpguss never helped when someone got stuck on a word.

And he always looked worried when they were reading.

"Tuck here figured it out the second day," Mr. Stumpguss said. "I got snookered into this."

Seth blinked. "Snookered?"

Mr. Stumpguss smiled. "Tricked, sort of. Tricked by my own pride."

Mr. Stumpguss took off his hat.

He put it back on.

"I signed a paper," he said. "Thought it was just a paper saying senior citizens should help out at school. Turns out it was a paper to go and do it."

"He couldn't read it," Tuck explained. "So he just signed it. And now Mrs. Fox wants him to read to us."

"You suppose maybe she'll forget?" Mr. Stumpguss asked.

He sounded hopeful.

"You don't know Mrs. Fox," Tuck said.

Seth nodded.

When Mrs. Fox said she was going to do something, she almost always did it.

"But if you tell her you can't read . . ." Seth said.

Tuck shook her head hard. "He doesn't want to do that."

"Why didn't your teacher help you learn?" Seth asked.

Mr. Stumpguss reached out and patted Seth's head. "I only went to school for a couple of years off and on. Dad needed me on the ranch. I learned how to count and figure from him. I can sign my name. I just never learned to write, or read."

Mr. Stumpguss was looking over their heads.

Seth tried to imagine what it would be like not to be able to read.

You wouldn't be able to read books.

Or letters from anyone.

You couldn't even read street signs. Or newspapers. And there was a test that drivers had to take.

A test you had to read.

"How can you drive?" Seth asked. "The driver's test, I mean."

"My sister helped me," Mr. Stumpguss said.

He was rubbing his hands together.

"She read the driver's book over and over until

I knew it by heart. Then she got a copy of the driver's test."

Mr. Stumpguss was almost whispering.

He was looking right at Seth.

"It wasn't cheating. I knew that book up, down, and sideways. Sis gave me the test out loud and I got every one right. A hundred percent. Then I memorized which ones to mark."

Seth didn't know what to say.

It *was* cheating, in a way. But Mr. Stumpguss didn't want to cheat. He just had to do things differently because he couldn't read.

"I know," Tuck said suddenly. "We'll teach you how to read."

Seth nodded, then he shook his head. "But we're the worst readers in the whole class, Tuck."

"And we don't have time," Mr. Stumpguss added. "Teacher wants me to read the story next week."

Tuck looked down at her shoes.

Seth felt bad. Mr. Stumpguss looked really upset.

Then Seth got an idea.

He pointed at the book in Mr. Stumpguss's hand.

"Tuck and I could read a story over and over until you learn it by heart, like the driver's book. You can pretend that you're reading."

Tuck looked up at Mr. Stumpguss. "Seth's right. You could do it. Please?"

Mr. Stumpguss laughed softly. "You don't give up, do you, Tuck?"

Tuck grinned at him and shook her head. "You always say it's not right to give up."

Mr. Stumpguss took off his hat, then put it back on.

"All right," he said. "It won't hurt anything as far as I can see."

"Yay!" Tuck yelled.

Seth grinned.

Mr. Stumpguss smiled.

His eyes got crinkly. He didn't look upset anymore.

"Give me the book," Tuck said. "I'll pick an easy story tonight. Tomorrow we'll meet you here after school."

Seth nodded. "We stay after school to play sometimes anyway."

Tuck was still smiling. "All the teachers leave right after school. No one will see us."

Mr. Stumpguss handed Tuck the book. "Don't lose it. You'll get me in trouble with Teacher if you do."

Tuck smiled. "I won't. I promise."

Mr. Stumpguss laughed. "It ought to work. I'm good at memorizing. And I can't see how it would do any harm if we snooker Mrs. Fox."

The bell rang.

"Time to go in," Mr. Stumpguss said.

Tuck pushed the book under her shirt.

They walked slowly back to class.

Seth saw Tuck slide the book into her backpack when Mrs. Fox wasn't looking.

6
SECRET READERS

Tuesday morning Seth told his mother he was going to stay after school with Tuck.

He told his mother Mr. Stumpguss would be there.

She knew all about Mr. Stumpguss.

Seth had told her about his stories.

She had seen the bobcat picture made with beans and seeds.

He didn't tell her about Mr. Stumpguss not being able to read.

Tuck was right.

He could keep a secret.

His mother said she would stop at the playground and meet Mr. Stumpguss on her way to the grocery store.

At school, Mr. Stumpguss helped Mrs. Fox the way he always did.

Seth watched him when they were reading.

Now that he knew Mr. Stumpguss couldn't read, he understood a lot of things.

He knew why Mr. Stumpguss frowned.

He knew why Mr. Stumpguss moved his lips and ran his finger underneath the words.

He was pretending to read.

At recess, Mr. Stumpguss told them the story about the big colt.

Dana and Ben sat down by the fence to listen.

Other kids sat down, too.

It was a long story.

The colt had broken down the corral fence three times. He had broken ropes and he bucked off everyone who tried to ride him.

Finally, the colt had gotten caught in fence wire.

Mr. Stumpguss had to cut the wire to free him.

After that, the colt let Mr. Stumpguss ride him.

Sort of, anyway.

"He was grateful to me for cutting him out of the wire," Mr. Stumpguss said. He took his hat off and put it back on. "But not that grateful."

The horse would let him get on, but at least once during the day, he would buck.

"Sometimes it would be first thing," Mr. Stumpguss said. "Other times he'd wait until noon. One day I thought he was going to forget, but he remembered. Bucked me off last thing, right as I was going back to the corral at dinnertime."

Everyone laughed.

Mr. Stumpguss laughed, too.

After recess they drew maps.

When the lunch bell rang, Mr. Stumpguss winked. "I'll see you after school."

Tuck and Seth watched him drive away.

The afternoon seemed longer than usual.

Mrs. Fox was teaching them about subtraction.

Finally, the bell rang.

After school, Seth and Tuck went out on the playground.

Kids yelled on their way to the buses.

Teachers got in their cars and drove away.

When everyone was gone, Tuck opened her backpack.

She got out the book.

"Which story did you pick?" Seth asked her.

She sat in a swing and opened the book. "This one."

Seth took the book from her.

"The Important Errand" was the title of the story.

Seth wasn't sure what the word *errand* meant. He asked Tuck.

She waved a hand at the cars going by "My mother calls it doing errands when we go shopping and stuff."

Seth flipped the pages.

It was pretty short.

Five pages.

The writing was small, though.

"It's the shortest one," Tuck said. She was watching the street. "I wish Mr. Stumpguss would come."

Seth looked toward the parking lot.

Then he looked at the book again.

He started reading.

Some of the words were sort of hard.

Tuck poked his shoulder.

Seth looked up. "I'm a little late," Mr. Stumpguss called. He was at the gate in the fence. He walked toward them.

Tuck jumped up.

"I was afraid you weren't going to come," she said.

Mr. Stumpguss smiled at her. "I said I would come, didn't I?"

He hadn't worn his hat. He didn't have his black suit on either.

His shirt was soft, like pajamas.

It was plaid, gray and blue.

He had a big belt buckle like a cowboy.

Tuck grinned at him. "I picked a story."

Mr. Stumpguss looked around. He walked to the merry-go-round and sat on the edge.

Seth and Tuck sat on each side of him.

He smelled even more minty than usual.

"Well, let's see it," he said.

Seth opened the book to "The Important Errand" and handed it to Mr. Stumpguss.

Mr. Stumpguss spread his fingers.

He touched the page. "Letters look like birdpecks to me. Hope you two can figure it out."

"We can," Tuck said.

She took the book from Mr. Stumpguss and started reading out loud.

Seth listened.

Tuck read faster than usual.

She really was reading better. Maybe she had been practicing at home, so she could help Dana and Ben when Mr. Stumpguss couldn't.

Maybe he should start practicing.

Tuck sounded pretty good.

There were only two words Tuck couldn't get.

Seth looked at them.

He couldn't figure them out either.

The story was different from the stories in their books.

The people in it lived on a farm. They had a wagon and a horse to pull it. They had candles instead of electric lights.

In the story, the boy was going to town to sell milk from their cow.

On the way, he spilled the milk.

He went to town anyway and got a job sweeping out a store.

He earned enough money to pay for the milk.

At the end of the story, there was a word printed in big letters in the middle of the page.

MORAL

Seth sounded it out, but he didn't know what it meant.

"That's the lesson in the story," Mr. Stumpguss said. "It's what you're supposed to learn. What's it say?"

Seth bent over the page. "It says, 'One mistake, a failure does not make.' "

It sounded backwards.

He looked up at Mr. Stumpguss.

"That means you can goof once and still straighten things out," he explained. "Like the boy. Spilled the milk, but then he got the job. See?"

Mr. Stumpguss was smiling.

His cottony hair was moving in the breeze. "It's true. Got to pick up and go on after you make mistakes. Got to be brave."

Tuck read the story again.

Mr. Stumpguss listened very carefully.

They tried to get the two words they hadn't figured out the first time.

They still couldn't.

Then Seth read the story. Mr. Stumpguss closed his eyes to listen better.

"What are dry goods?" Seth asked when he was finished. The store the boy had swept out was called a dry-goods store.

"Cloth, thread and needles, buttons," Mr. Stumpguss told him. "Used to be a dry-goods store in every town."

Seth heard a horn honk.

His mother was pulling into the parking lot.

She got out of the car.

"That's my mother," Seth said. "She wants to meet you. I didn't tell her what we're doing."

Mr. Stumpguss stood up. He walked toward Seth's mother.

Seth watched them shake hands.

He could see his mother smiling.

He wondered what she would say if she knew Mr. Stumpguss couldn't read.

Tuck grabbed his arm.

"Take this," she said. She was handing him the book. "Get your mom to read those two words."

Seth took the book and walked across the grass.

His mother and Mr. Stumpguss were talking about how nice and warm the weather had been.

Seth found the first word.

"Mom?" he asked.

She looked at him.

"What's this word?"

She glanced at the book. "*Disappointed*."

"And this one?" He pointed at the other hard word.

"That one is *responsibility*," she said. Then she was looking at the book more closely.

"Where did that book come from?" she asked. "It's old, isn't it?"

Seth nodded. He held his breath. He hadn't thought about what to say about the book.

He didn't like pretending or lying.

"Mrs. Fox loaned it to me," Mr. Stumpguss said.

He felt for his hat, but it wasn't there.

"How nice," Seth's mother said. "And you're reading them the stories?"

"We're reading to him," Seth said quickly.

It was true.

And he hadn't told her Mr. Stumpguss's secret.

"Good for you," his mother said.

She looked at Mr. Stumpguss. "Is Seth's reading improving?"

Mr. Stumpguss felt for his hat again. He touched his hair instead.

"I think so," he said, finally.

His voice sounded different, the way it had with Mrs. Fox. His eyes weren't crinkly even though he was smiling.

Seth's mother said good-bye to Mr. Stumpguss. She told Seth to come home in an hour or so.

Seth watched her leave.

Mr. Stumpguss was frowning.

He has to tell little lies all the time, Seth thought. *He has to pretend all the time.*

It would be terrific if Mr. Stumpguss could really learn to read.

Then he could stop being worried that someone would find out.

"Let's get back to it," Mr. Stumpguss said.

They went back to the merry-go-round.

Seth read the story.

Then Tuck did.

Then it was Seth's turn again.

Mr. Stumpguss tried to repeat parts of the story.

He could almost repeat the first page when it was time to go home.

"We're going to snooker everyone," Tuck said.

Mr. Stumpguss laughed.

He patted Seth's shoulder. He thanked them for helping him.

Then he got in his big black car and drove away.

7 THE MOST AWFUL STORY

By Friday morning, Mr. Stumpguss knew the whole story.

He could say it from the beginning to the end.

He never made a mistake.

They had even taught him when to turn the pages.

He was ready.

Mrs. Fox looked really happy when he told her he would read the story that day.

"Reading groups first," she said to the class. "Then we get to hear a story from Mr. Stumpguss."

Kids cheered.

They went to the tables in the back of the room.

While the Bobcats read out loud, Seth saw Mr. Stumpguss's lips moving.

Seth knew what he was doing.

He wasn't pretending to read this time.

He was practicing.

"You know the story really well," Seth whispered to Mr. Stumpguss when reading groups were over.

Mr. Stumpguss was turning his hat around and around.

"You'll snooker everyone," Tuck said quietly.

Seth could tell she was trying to smile.

But she looked nervous.

Mr. Stumpguss's hat was going in circles so fast that watching it made Seth feel sort of sick.

"Are you ready, Mr. Stumpguss?" Mrs. Fox said from the front of the room.

Mr. Stumpguss looked up at her.

"Yes," he said.

He was already holding the book.

He had been holding it under his arm all morning.

He had marked the right page.

He walked to the front of the room and stood by Mrs. Fox's desk.

She was smiling and her eyebrows were up.

Seth and Tuck slid into their seats.

"Everyone listen now," Mrs. Fox said in her smooth, deep, important voice. The noise in the room died down.

Mr. Stumpguss held the book up high and started the story.

He held the book in one hand.

His hat was in his other hand.

At first everything was fine.

Mr. Stumpguss moved his eyes. It really looked like he was reading.

Seth held his breath.

Mr. Stumpguss was saying the words a little too slowly, but that was okay.

Then he started going faster.

By the time he got to the part about the boy milking the cow, he was going way too fast. It was hard to understand what he was saying.

Ben started looking in his pack. Dana was drawing. Some of the other kids started whispering.

Mrs. Fox's lips got stiff, but she didn't say anything. She stared at the kids who were whispering until they saw her and got quiet again.

Someone giggled.

Mr. Stumpguss looked over the top of the book.

He kept talking.

Seth looked at Tuck.

She was waving her hand back and forth.

Seth wondered what she was doing. Then he figured it out.

Mr. Stumpguss had forgotten to turn to the second page. Tuck was trying to remind him.

Mr. Stumpguss saw her. He jerked his eyes back to the book and tried to turn the page.

But he was still holding his hat.

It slid across the page.

Mr. Stumpguss looked around for a place to set his hat down. He was still talking.

Now he was saying the words way too slowly again.

He finally shoved his hat under his arm.

He shoved it too hard. It almost fell, but he mashed it between his arm and his side. Suddenly the book snapped shut and he dropped it. His glasses slid down to the end of his nose.

Mrs. Fox was staring at him.

Kids were giggling.

They were whispering.

Mr. Stumpguss didn't stop reciting the story, even while he was bending over to get the book.

As he picked it up, his hat fell out from under his arm. His glasses slipped off and fell to the floor.

He tried to catch his hat. He dropped the book again.

He didn't stop talking, though. He went right on talking as he crammed his hat into his suit pocket.

He was still telling the story, but it sure didn't look like he was reading anymore.

He picked up the book. He picked up his glasses and put them back on.

He had gotten to the part of the story about the boy seeing the dry-goods store.

Mr. Stumpguss started flipping pages.

He couldn't find the right one, but he kept talking. The boy in the story was asking for a job.

Mr. Stumpguss was almost at the end.

He was still trying to find the right page.

He got to the moral.

He was still turning the pages, but he said the moral anyway.

Then he was quiet, looking down at the book.

His hat was mashed flat, sticking out of his pocket.

His face was red.

His hair was all fluffed up from bending over.

He finally shook his head and closed the book.

Tuck made a funny little sound, like she was about to cry.

Mr. Stumpguss looked up at Mrs. Fox.

"I'm sorry," he said. He set the book carefully on her desk. Then he walked right out of the room.

Tuck covered her face with her hands.

Seth felt like crying, too. They hadn't snookered anyone.

All they had done was make Mr. Stumpguss feel awful.

Mrs. Fox got up. Her lips were so stiff they looked like they might crack if she tried to talk.

"Behave until I get back," she said over her shoulder. She said it in her smoothest, deepest, most important voice.

She went out into the hallway.

Kids got quiet.

Everyone was staring at the doorway.

"Is Mr. Stumpguss weird or what?" Seth heard someone whisper. Kids laughed.

A paper airplane flew across the back of the room.

Tuck jumped up. "Shut up," she yelled at the whole class. "You all just shut up!"

Everyone got really quiet.

Tuck turned to look at Seth. "Come on," she said.

She didn't look at anyone. Her chin was way up. It was almost pointing at the ceiling. She walked out the door.

Seth got up and followed her.

"You'll get in trouble," Ben said as Seth passed him.

Seth kept walking.

The hall was empty.

He could hear other teachers talking to their classes.

The hall seemed too wide. It seemed too long.

Their footsteps sounded too loud.

"We're going to get in trouble," Seth said.

"I don't care," Tuck whispered as they went out the big doors onto the steps. "Do you?"

Seth shook his head.

It wasn't quite true. He did care about getting in trouble. But he cared more about Mr. Stumpguss.

A lot more.

They saw Mrs. Fox in front of the school.

She was watching Mr. Stumpguss drive away.

Tuck started running.

Seth did too.

They ran their fastest, but Mr. Stumpguss turned the corner without seeing them.

He was gone.

When Mrs. Fox turned and saw them, she frowned. "What do you two think you're doing?"

Seth looked at her.

Her whole face was stiff.

Her lips looked like they were made out of cement.

Seth thought about having cement lips.

For a second he was afraid he would laugh. Or start crying. He felt really mixed-up.

Tuck's eyes were wide and shiny. "Mr. Stumpguss will come back, won't he?"

Mrs. Fox's lips got soft again. Then her whole face got soft. "I don't know, Tuck," she said. "He just kept saying he was sorry."

"We shouldn't have made him do it," Tuck said suddenly.

Mrs. Fox shook her head. "I had no idea he would get that nervous, Tuck. He was so nervous he had memorized the whole story. Could you tell?"

"He memorized it because he can't read," Tuck almost shouted.

Mrs. Fox blinked twice. "He what?"

"He can't read," Seth said miserably.

He wondered if Mr. Stumpguss would be mad at them for telling his secret.

"Oh, my," Mrs. Fox said. "Oh, my, oh, my."

Tuck looked at her. "He never went to school except off and on for two years."

"He had to work on his father's ranch," Seth said.

"Oh, my," Mrs. Fox said again. "Then who helped him learn the story? You two? During reading groups?"

Seth shook his head. "After school."

Tuck kicked at the ground. "We wanted to snooker everyone."

Mrs. Fox looked puzzled. "Snooker?"

"Mr. Stumpguss says that," Seth said. "It means tricking someone, sort of. I think."

"Mr. Stumpguss has to snooker people all the time," Tuck said, "to make them think he can read."

Seth looked at Mrs. Fox. "I wish he could be a Bobcat. We could help him learn to read."

Mrs. Fox was nodding slowly.

She kept nodding for a minute.

"You two go back to class," she said. "Tell everyone to settle down. Tell them I'll be right back."

She walked away, heading for the office.

She was walking fast.

Her shoe heels made clacking noises on the sidewalk.

Seth and Tuck went back to Mrs. Fox's room.

Kids were noisy, but everyone was sitting down.

"Mrs. Fox will be right back," Tuck said loudly. "She said to settle down." Then she plopped into her desk seat.

Seth went to the back row.

Kids were looking at him.

They were all wondering what had happened.

The room got quieter.

He could hear Ben's potato-chip bag crinkling.

When Mrs. Fox came back, she was smiling. "I think things might work out," she said, looking at Tuck, then over the other kids' heads at Seth. "We'll know Monday."

That was all she would tell them.

Walking home from school, Seth kicked pebbles on the sidewalk.

Tuck kept stamping her feet.

Seth knew what she was thinking.

They might never see Mr. Stumpguss again.

8

A REAL THIRD GRADER

Monday morning Seth started walking to school early.

Tuck was already ahead of him.

He yelled for her to wait, but she didn't slow down.

He ran to catch up.

Tuck looked at him.

"Ben will think we're both sick when he finally gets going," Seth said.

Tuck didn't answer.

He didn't know what else to say, so he didn't say anything.

They went around the corner, walking fast.

They crossed the playground.

Tuck ran up the steps and Seth followed her.

There were only a few kids in the hall.

They were really early.

Tuck stopped in front of room 27.

She took a deep breath.

"I just hope he's here," Seth said.

Tuck nodded. She opened the door.

They went in.

The folding chair at the back of the room was empty.

Mrs. Fox looked up from her desk. "You two are early. I bet I know why." She smiled at them. "I talked to Mr. Stumpguss on Saturday. I told him the principal said he could come to class to learn to read, starting today."

Seth looked at Mrs. Fox. "Mr. Stumpguss could be a real third grader? He could be a Bobcat?"

Mrs. Fox nodded.

"But that doesn't mean he will," Tuck said.

"No, it doesn't," Mrs. Fox said. "But he might."

Seth tried to smile.

Tuck didn't say anything. She went and sat in her desk. She slid way down in her seat. She kept watching the door.

Other kids came in. It got noisy. Then the bell rang.

Ben came in last.

Everyone looked at the empty folding chair at the back of the room.

"I'm not sure whether Mr. Stumpguss will be coming today," Mrs. Fox told the class. "But if he does, I want everyone to behave. I want everyone to be very, very nice to him."

All the kids were quiet.

Seth could tell that they felt bad for laughing at Mr. Stumpguss.

Tuck was turned in her seat.

She was still looking at the door.

"Reading groups," Mrs. Fox said. Her voice sounded too soft. She sounded sad.

Seth pulled his reading book out of his desk.

Papers fell on the floor.

He bent to pick them up.

He thought about the first day that Mr. Stumpguss had come.

He had looked funny sitting in the desk.

Seth walked to the Bobcat table.

Tuck was already there. So were Ben and Dana.

They started reading.

Seth read without getting stuck.

So did Ben.

Dana took his turn, then Tuck read. Tuck kept looking up at the door and losing her place.

Mr. Stumpguss didn't come.

After reading groups, Mrs. Fox gave them an art project. They used string to make pictures.

Seth tried to make another bobcat. It didn't come out very well.

Then the recess bell rang.

Everyone lined up.

Tuck still looked upset and sad. Mrs. Fox walked with her arm around Tuck's shoulders. At the top of the steps, Mrs. Fox stopped. Tuck kept walking.

Kids yelled to her but she acted like she didn't hear them.

Seth followed Tuck onto the playground.

Maybe if they played the monster game, Tuck would feel better.

But maybe not.

He didn't really feel like running around screaming, either.

"Tuck?" he called, but she just kept walking, looking at the ground. He ran to catch up with her. Then he saw Mr. Stumpguss over by the fence.

He smacked Tuck's shoulder. She turned around. She looked like she was about to punch him.

"Look," Seth said. He pointed. "Mr. Stumpguss is here."

Tuck whirled around and started running.

Seth tried to keep up.

They both pounded up to Mr. Stumpguss.

He was smiling. He had on his soft shirt, and his hair was fluffy.

"Had to come and say good-bye to you two," he said.

Tuck hugged him. He patted her hair. Then she stood back.

Mr. Stumpguss squeezed Seth's shoulders. Then he hugged him, too.

"I'm going to miss you two," Mr. Stumpguss said.

"Why won't you come and learn to read?" Tuck asked.

Mr. Stumpguss shook his head.

He didn't say anything.

"You could be a Bobcat," Seth said. "We're all slow readers. We're the worst."

Mr. Stumpguss laughed. His eyes got crinkly.

Seth tried to think of something else to say. Mr. Stumpguss looked like he felt a little better.

"Reading isn't that hard," Seth said.

Tuck nodded. "I hardly ever get stuck anymore."

"We would help you," Seth promised.

Mr. Stumpguss was looking at them, smiling a little.

"You could try," Tuck said. "You could at least be brave and try."

"The moral said that one mistake doesn't mean you have to give up," Seth said. "You told us it was true."

"You tell me to be brave all the time," Tuck said, stamping her foot. "Besides, it won't be that hard."

Mr. Stumpguss laughed again. "You two know what you're doing, don't you?" he asked.

Tuck nodded.

Seth nodded too. "We're snookering you," he said.

Mr. Stumpguss looked at them. "You sure are."

"Does that mean you'll do it?" Tuck asked him.

He shook his head.

"None of the Bobcats would make fun of you," Tuck said.

Seth nodded. "And if you learned to read you could stop lying and pretending all the time."

Mr. Stumpguss was quiet.

Seth couldn't think of anything else to say.

Then Mr. Stumpguss reached out and laid his hands lightly on Seth's shoulders. "They gave me heck at the Senior Citizen Center when I told them I was quitting," he said. "I told them it was too much for me, getting here early every day."

He was looking at Seth.

Seth tried not to blink.

"You're right, Seth," Mr. Stumpguss said in a very soft voice. "Lying and pretending are hard."

A bunch of kids ran by.

They all yelled hello to Mr. Stumpguss.

"Why weren't you here this morning, Mr. Stumpguss?" Dana hollered. He was grinning.

Ben was being a monster.

He roared and chased Dana. Dana ran all the way around Mr. Stumpguss, trying to get away.

Mr. Stumpguss laughed.

Ben roared again.

Everyone ran to the other side of the playground.

"Please," Tuck said quietly.

Mr. Stumpguss reached up like he was going to take his hat off.

But he didn't have it on.

He touched his cottony hair instead.

Then he looked at Tuck and Seth.

"All right," Mr. Stumpguss said. "Last chance I'm likely to get, isn't it? Let's go tell Teacher."

He walked toward the steps.

Tuck pounded Seth on the back.

They ran in circles around Mr. Stumpguss the whole way across the playground.

The bell rang as they got to the doors.

Mr. Stumpguss stopped.

Kids were running past them into the hall.

"I'm a little scared, you know," Mr. Stumpguss said.

"Don't be," Tuck said. She took his hand and held it. Seth took his other hand.

They went up the steps together.

Mrs. Fox was at her desk.

"Mr. Stumpguss is back," Seth told her. He was grinning. He felt wonderful.

Mrs. Fox smiled. Her eyebrows went way up. "Reading groups," she said to the class.

"But we already had reading groups," Dana said.

Mrs. Fox smiled again.

"I know," she said. "But someone special was missing."

She explained that Mr. Stumpguss had never learned to read. She told everyone that he was going to be a Bobcat.

Everyone yelled and cheered.

Mr. Stumpguss looked at the class. "Well, come on, come on," he said. "Let's get to work."

Seth got his reading book out of his desk.

He saw Tuck getting some white cards from Mrs. Fox. He remembered them from first grade.

Each card had a letter printed on it.

Seth smiled.

He felt terrific.

Mr. Stumpguss was already at the Bobcat table, and he was smiling, too.